Buried Alive!

Buried Alive!

by
Charlene Anderson

Beacon Hill Press of Kansas City
Kansas City, Missouri

Copyright 2003
by Beacon Hill Press of Kansas City

Printed in the United States of America

ISBN 083-412-0100

Cover Design: Ted Ferguson
Illustrator: Ted Ferguson

Editor: Donna Manning
Assistant Editor: Stephanie Harris

Note: This is a fictional story based on the earthquake of 2001 in Lima, Peru. It is part of the *Understanding Christian Mission,* Children's Mission Education curriculum. It is designed to correlate with this year's theme, Compassionate Ministries. Lessons focus on how missionaries help people meet their physical, emotional, and spiritual needs.

10 9 8 7 6 5 4 3 2 1

Contents

1

Rescued

"It's an earthquake!" someone yelled. "Get away from the building!"

The factory whistle began to blow. I turned to see the doors burst open. Workmen were running out in all directions.

I had just been inside to drop off my brother's lunch and was heading home. All of a sudden, I felt the ground move.

"John!" I screamed for my brother, but I didn't see him among the workmen.

I was so scared. But all I could do was stand and watch as the earth split wide open. The other side of the ground moved up and away from me.

"Head for cover!" I heard a man cry.

Just then, I saw a big piece of wall falling toward me. I quickly dove into a nearby ditch and curled up into a ball. I covered my head and waited.

I heard mud bricks tumbling down all

around me. They sounded like bowling balls slamming against one another.

As I lay in the ditch, the earth continued to rumble and sway. When it finally stopped, I tried to get up. But I could not move. I was trapped—buried under a wall of mud bricks. I panicked and gasped for air. Instead of air, I got a mouth and nose full of gritty dust. I coughed and coughed.

I could hear people yelling and running around above me. I screamed, "Help!" as loud as I could. But no one responded.

Then I realized I could move. I tried pushing up on the wall, but it would not budge. I was alone and afraid.

I screamed again, "Help! Help!" Still, no one came to help.

Suddenly, I heard a man's voice. "Can you hear me?" he called.

"Yes!" I exclaimed. "Please help me! Hurry!"

"We will. We'll have you out in no time." The man's voice was kind, yet firm. "Don't give up!" he shouted.

I could hear people working above me. It seemed to take them forever. But after a few minutes, they gently pulled me from the ditch. I found myself surrounded by a man, a woman, a teenage girl, and a boy who looked like he was about my age.

"Gracias (thank you)." I coughed and tried to blink the dust from my eyes.

"Are you hurt?" the man asked, extending his hand. He slowly pulled me up.

I raised and lowered my shoulders. Then I twisted from side to side. "I don't think I'm hurt, but I sure am sore."

"What's your name, son?" the man asked.

"My name is Paulo."

"My name is Ron," the man said, "and this is my wife, Judy, my son, Gregg, and my daughter, Emily. We're missionaries here in Lima [LEE-muh], Peru."

"It's a miracle we heard you," said Judy.

"But I'm glad we did." Gregg smiled.

"Me too," I said.

"Where do you live, Paulo?" asked Emily.

"I live in Youngtown. But my brother, John, works here at the factory. That's why I'm in Lima. I had just dropped off his lunch and was heading home when the factory whistle blew. Everyone ran outside, but I didn't see John."

"Maybe he went home," said Ron. "We'll walk with you to Youngtown and help you find John and your parents."

"You need to see a doctor," suggested Judy, "just to be sure you're all right."

"No doctor. No! No! I can't pay."

Just then, the ground began to rumble and roll again.

"Oh, I feel sick." I held my stomach.

"The ground is rolling like an ocean," said Emily.

"It really is, Dad. Look!" Gregg shouted. "Let's get out of here, like fast!"

"Si (yes)!" I yelled. "No more ditches, please."

Gregg helped me as we walked past groups of people rushing in the opposite direction.

"Hey, you're going the wrong way. Haven't you heard?" someone shouted as they hurried past us.

"Heard what?" I yelled.

"Hey, Dad," called Gregg. "Turn on your radio. Let's find out what he's talking about."

We soon heard the news. "The earthquake has caused much damage in Lima, and it has destroyed Youngtown!"

2

Finding a Treasure

"Oh no!" I buried my head in my hands and tried hard not to cry. I began to realize this news was about my house, my family, and me.

"I-I can't believe it. I've got to get home! I've got to find my family!" I said to Gregg as we walked a little faster.

"We'll help you, Paulo." Judy tried to comfort me.

The ground continued to tremble as we approached Youngtown, located on the outskirts of Lima.

"Did you feel the ground moving?" I asked. "It's scary. Every time the earth shakes, I get a creepy feeling all over me."

"Me too," nodded Gregg.

"Don't worry," Ron said. "The worst is over."

"I hope so!" exclaimed Emily.

When we reached Youngtown, we discovered the news reports were correct. Nothing was left standing on the street where I lived.

My house was a pile of rocks, boards, and strips of tin. Broken dishes, dented pans, clothes, and toys were scattered everywhere.

Someone's doll looked up at me from under a twisted piece of metal. I cleared off a place and sat down.

"Mama, Papa, John, where are you?" I whispered. "I don't know what to do."

"Scoot over, Paulo." Gregg sat down beside me.

"It's sure a mess, isn't it?" I sat quietly and looked at the debris.

"It's awful," agreed Gregg.

As Gregg sat and kicked at the small rocks by his feet, he saw something shiny on the ground. "What's this?" he asked.

"My flute!" I exclaimed. "You found my flute! Thank you. Thank you."

I took off the mouthpiece and shook out the dirt. "I hope it still works. I'll have to clean it up before I can try it."

Gregg's dad came over and stood beside us.

"Look what Gregg found," I said as I held up my flute.

"We have one at the church you can play if your flute doesn't work," Ron said.

"That makes me feel better. I love to play the flute," I said.

"Paulo, we are going to help you find your family," said Judy. "But right now, we would like to invite you to come home with us. You can get cleaned up, change clothes, and rest. You can stay as long as you want."

"Please come, Paulo," urged Gregg.

"Will my family be able to find me at your house?"

"We'll call and leave our phone number with those in charge," explained Ron. "That way, they will be able to find you. We'll bring you back tomorrow and begin our search for your family. But right now, we must get to our house."

3

Gregg's Idea

"It's all set," Ron said walking into the kitchen. "We're going to set up a tent with the other missionaries from Lima. Then we will be able to distribute supplies to the earthquake victims."

"Oh, that's great!" replied Judy.

"Ummm. Something smells delicious!" Ron sniffed the air. "Emily, go tell the boys to come and eat."

Gregg's mom had fixed homemade soup while I cleaned up. I had never taken a bath in a tub before, but I did not tell Gregg. I did tell him I was hungry. So when Emily called, I was ready to eat. As we enjoyed our soup, I talked with Gregg about his family.

"What are missionaries?" I asked.

"Missionaries are called by God to teach people in other cultures about His love," Gregg explained. "One way they share God's love is by helping people in need. Mom and Dad enjoy being missionaries and helping others."

After Gregg and I finished our soup, he took me to his room. "I have an idea," Gregg said, as he reached under his bed and pulled out three brightly-colored bags. One was blue, one was red-orange, and one was green.

"I want to help people too." Gregg placed the bags on his bed and opened them. "A lady at my church made these for me," he said. "They are just what I need. I will fill them with food for the earthquake victims."

"While I'm waiting for your dad to take me back to Youngtown, I can help you," offered Paulo.

"That would be great! I was hoping you would want to help me," said Gregg.

"But where will we get the food?" I asked.

"We'll collect it by going door-to-door. If Dad gives us the OK, we can begin tomorrow."

Just then, the doorbell rang.

Gregg's mother called, "Get the door, will you, Gregg? Duke is coming to visit Emily."

"Come on, Paulo," Gregg said. "I want you to meet this guy. He works at a radio station in Lima."

"Nice to meet you, Paulo," Duke said.

"I'm glad to meet you too," I replied.

"Paulo lost everything in the quake, including his family," explained Gregg.

Duke held out his hand to me. "I'm very sorry. If there is anything I can do, please let me know."

"Thanks," I said. There were tears in my eyes, but I did not want anyone to see me cry.

When we returned to Gregg's room, I noticed my flute had been cleaned.

"Mom did it." Gregg smiled.

When his mom came to say goodnight, I thanked her.

"Play a tune for us." She handed me the flute.

"Yes, Paulo," pleaded Gregg.

When I first blew into the mouthpiece, the notes squeaked. But soon they were steady and clear.

Judy and Gregg clapped. "Do you have a teacher?" asked Judy.

"No. I taught myself how to play, and I made up the tune."

"Wow! That's cool!" exclaimed Gregg.

"You play very well," commented Judy. "Now it is time for you to get some rest."

Gregg's dad heard the music and came to

tell us goodnight. "Are you all right?" he asked me.

"I feel very sad," I admitted.

"Of course you do," Ron said. "Let's pray about it."

"OK." I nodded my head.

"Thank you, God, for leading us to Paulo. Help him to feel better, and help us find his family. Amen."

I did feel better after Ron prayed. Gregg let me sleep on the top bunk. I could not wait to tell Mama, Papa, and John. "I must find them. I will find them!" I thought as I drifted off to sleep.

The next morning, I helped Gregg and his parents load the van. "Where did you get all this food and clothing?" I asked.

"The church collects food and clothing all year long. That way, we have it for times like this," explained Judy.

"Let's go," called Ron. "Gregg, don't forget the bags for collecting your food."

"I've got them, Dad. Paulo, here's your flute," said Gregg.

"Thanks! I'll play it as I search for Mama and Papa. They know my music. It might help me find them."

As soon as Gregg's parents and the other missionaries set up the tent, people lined up in front of it. Gregg's parents worked steadily until noon.

In the meantime, Gregg and I went door-to-door to ask for food donations. The earthquake did not ruin all of the homes in Lima. So many people shared what they had. We returned to the tent with all three bags filled.

We were glad to help those who needed food. And we realized that even young people can do their part.

"Paulo, we're going with you to search for your family now," said Ron. "But first, let's join hands and pray."

As Ron prayed, I stood quietly and listened. I believed God was listening too. I also believed He was going to answer our prayer.

"Paulo!" a voice shouted. "Paulo! I've been looking everywhere for you!"

4

An Answer to Prayer

"I thought I'd never see you again!" I cried, running toward John. My brother grabbed my arms, swung me around and around, and gave me a big hug. It felt so good to see my brother and know I still had family.

"What about Mama and Papa?" I asked. "Have you seen them?"

"No. I've been looking all night."

I buried my face in his shirt. He held me tight. Then, I remembered my new friends. "This is Ron and Judy. They are missionaries. They were just praying that God would help us find my family," I said.

"I know. I heard them. That's how I found you."

"Praise the Lord!" Judy exclaimed.

"This is their son, Gregg. They saved my life. And they're going to help us find Mama and Papa," I added.

"Thanks for helping my brother," said

John. "I've looked everywhere I can think of for Mama and Papa."

"I have a few suggestions," said Ron.

We searched several places, but by the end of the day, we had not found Mama or Papa.

"Paulo, I want you to stay with Gregg again tonight. I'm staying overnight with a friend. I'll let you know if I find out anything more about Mama and Papa."

"I'll do that," I said.

Soon we were back at Gregg's house.

"I have another idea," Gregg said. "Today on the radio I heard a man talking to people on the street about the earthquake. Why couldn't Duke ask you and me questions about collecting the food? He did say he'd help."

"What a great idea," said Judy.

"I think he would do it," Emily said.

"It just might work," Ron agreed.

"Can we call him now?" Gregg asked excitedly.

"Tomorrow would be better," suggested Judy.

Early the next morning, Gregg called Duke to share his idea.

"Great idea!" exclaimed Duke. "Come on over."

"Yea! We're going to be on the radio!" the boys exclaimed.

✳ ✳ ✳

Duke asked Gregg and me many questions. When he finished, he invited me to come back and play my flute.

"People have already begun calling into the station," Duke said. "We are getting a good response! Many people who have not been hurt by the earthquake want to give food to those who need help, especially in Youngtown."

"Good job, Paulo." Gregg held out his hand to let me give it a slap.

"You did good, too, Gregg." I held out my hand in return.

"Well, boys, I have to get back to work," said Duke. "By the way, I forgot to give you this message."

"Listen to this." Gregg read out loud.

Dear Gregg and Paulo,

I'm the director at an orphanage. The boys and girls here want to help. Maybe we could work together to collect food.

Signed,

C. W. Jackson

"Is this guy for real?" asked Gregg.

"Yes," I said. "I've seen his orphanage. A lot of kids live there. Let's talk to your dad about this."

* * *

The boys and girls at the orphanage did go door-to-door with us. Ron and Judy followed us in the van. When we finished collecting the food, we took it to the tent for the missionaries to distribute.

5

Friends Forever

"I've found Mama and Papa!" John exclaimed as he rushed into the tent.

My heart beat so fast, I could barely speak.

John explained that Mama and Papa were in a hospital. "Mama hit her head and doesn't remember anything. Papa cries all day, but there's nothing physically wrong with him. Seeing you, Paulo, will help them, I'm sure."

Ron took us to the hospital. I ran to Mama's bed and played her favorite tune on my flute. Her eyes blinked.

"Mama! Mama!" I cried. "It's me, Paulo." I put my hand in hers. She squeezed it.

"Paulo, this is a good sign," said the doctor.

Ron winked at me. "God can do anything, Paulo. Never forget that."

"What about Papa?" asked John.

"He will be all right in time," answered the doctor.

"John, I believed God was going to help us find them, and He did. I've never believed like that before," I said.

"Faith is a wonderful gift, Paulo," smiled Judy as she gave me a hug.

"We will continue to help you and your family," offered Ron.

"Paulo can stay with us for as long as he wants," added Judy.

"Yippee!" exclaimed Gregg.

* * *

I sat in front of the microphone. Duke's wink was my cue to start.

"My name is Paulo Lopez. A lot of good things have happened since I last talked to you. I found my brother and my parents. We are helping the missionaries distribute food and supplies at the tent. And many friends are helping us to rebuild our house in Youngtown."

I turned the mike toward Gregg.

"My name is Gregg Robinson. Thank you for giving food to help others . . ."

Just then, a lady burst into the room. She handed something to Duke.

"Radio audience," Duke said, "I have two gold medals for two special young men. Thank you, Paulo and Gregg, for helping the people of Lima and Youngtown."

Duke hung a medal around my neck. Then he hung one around Gregg's neck. Gregg and I turned and looked at one another and grinned.

"Friends forever," Gregg said.

"Friends forever," I repeated.

OUT	Name	IN
7/13	Andrew Mittler ✓	8/17
8/17	Rachel Hansen ✓	8/17
8/17	Connie Sheehy ✓	8/17
8/17	Chrissy Michaels ✓	8/17
10/16	Alexis Antle ✓	10/16
11/12	Ashley Chase ✓	1/4/04
11/12	Brent Chase ✓	1/4/04
2/09	Gabe Rouley	3/21
2/09	~~Morgan Rouley~~ NO	
8/15	Jimmy D.	8/27
9/12	Gabe R.	9/12
5/8	William C	6/10

Buried Alive
#1